Where's Buddy?

Written by Alice Russ Watson

Illustrated by Roy Hermelin

Collins

What's in this story?

Listen and say 🎧

map

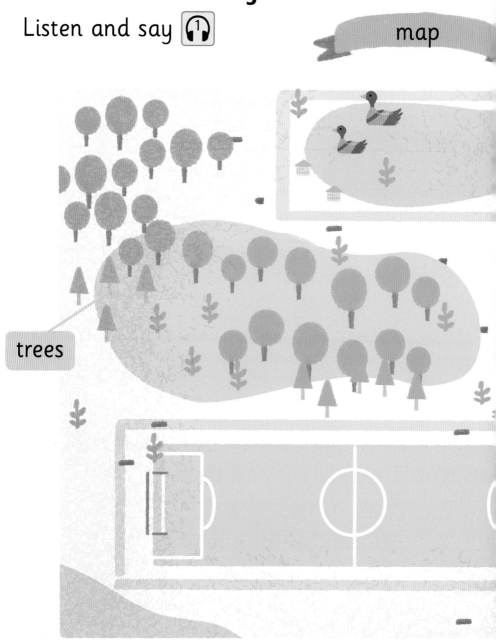

trees

Download the audio at www.collins.co.uk/839820

pond swings café

picnic table bin

🎧② Charlie and her dog, Buddy, are going to the park with Dad. Charlie and Buddy love the park.

In the car, Buddy sits next to Charlie.
He puts his head out of the window.
"Be careful, Buddy!" says Charlie.

At the park, they run and jump and play on the grass. Charlie can run very fast, but Buddy is faster!

Charlie sees her friend Reo and his dad.

"Hi, Reo," says Charlie.

"Hi, Charlie. Hi, Buddy," says Reo.

Buddy likes Reo.

"Do you want to play on the swings?"
asks Reo.

"OK," says Charlie. "Buddy, stay here.
You can't go on the swings."

"This is fun!" says Charlie.

"Yes, the swings are my favourite. I can go to the sky!" says Reo.

Charlie likes the swings, but she wants to play with Buddy.

"Let's go and see Buddy," says Charlie.

"Oh no! Where's Buddy?" says Charlie.

Charlie and Reo look for Buddy.

They look under the picnic tables, but they can't find him.

They look between the trees and they look behind the bins, but they can't find Buddy.

Charlie is very sad. She starts to cry.

Reo says, "I've got an idea! Let's draw a map of the park and look in all the different places for Buddy."

Reo draws a map of the park.

"Which way?" asks Reo.

"Let's go left," says Charlie.

Charlie and Reo go left. They see a girl climbing a tree and some children playing football, but they don't see Buddy.

"Let's go right," says Charlie.

Charlie and Reo go right. On the pond, they see a frog jumping and some ducks swimming, but they don't see Buddy.

"Let's go straight on," says Charlie.

Charlie and Reo go straight on. They see a family having a picnic and a boy eating an ice cream, but they don't see Buddy.

Charlie has an idea.

"Buddy loves ice cream," she says.
"Where's the café?"

Charlie and Reo look at their map.

"Let's go right, then left!" says Reo.

Charlie and Reo are at the café, and so is Buddy.

"There you are, Buddy!" says Charlie. She's very happy now.

"Would you like an ice cream?" asks Dad.
"Yes, please!" they say.

Picture dictionary

Listen and repeat

behind

between

go left

go right

go straight on

next to

under

1 Look and order the story

2 Listen and say

Collins

Published by Collins
An imprint of HarperCollins*Publishers*
Westerhill Road
Bishopbriggs
Glasgow
G64 2QT

HarperCollins*Publishers*
1st Floor, Watermarque Building
Ringsend Road
Dublin 4
Ireland

William Collins' dream of knowledge for all began with the publication of his first book in 1819.

A self-educated mill worker, he not only enriched millions of lives, but also founded a flourishing publishing house. Today, staying true to this spirit, Collins books are packed with inspiration, innovation and practical expertise. They place you at the centre of a world of possibility and give you exactly what you need to explore it.

© HarperCollins*Publishers* Limited 2020

10 9 8 7 6 5 4 3 2

ISBN 978-0-00-839820-0

Collins® and COBUILD® are registered trademarks of HarperCollins*Publishers* Limited

www.collins.co.uk/elt

British Library Cataloguing in Publication Data

A catalogue record for this publication is available from the British Library.

Author: Alice Russ Watson
Illustrator: Roy Hermelin (Beehive)
Series editor: Rebecca Adlard
Publishing manager: Lisa Todd
Product managers: Jennifer Hall and Caroline Green
In-house editor: Alma Puts Keren
Project manager: Emily Hooton
Editor: Matthew Hancock
Proofreaders: Natalie Murray and Michael Lamb
Cover designer: Kevin Robbins
Typesetter: 2Hoots Publishing Services Ltd
Audio produced by id audio, London
Reading guide author: Emma Wilkinson
Production controller: Rachel Weaver
Printed and bound by: GPS Group, Slovenia

MIX
Paper from
responsible sources

FSC
www.fsc.org

FSC™ C007454

This book is produced from independently certified FSC™ paper to ensure responsible forest management.

For more information visit: **www.harpercollins.co.uk/green**

Download the audio for this book and a reading guide for parents and teachers at www.collins.co.uk/839820